ZOMBIES

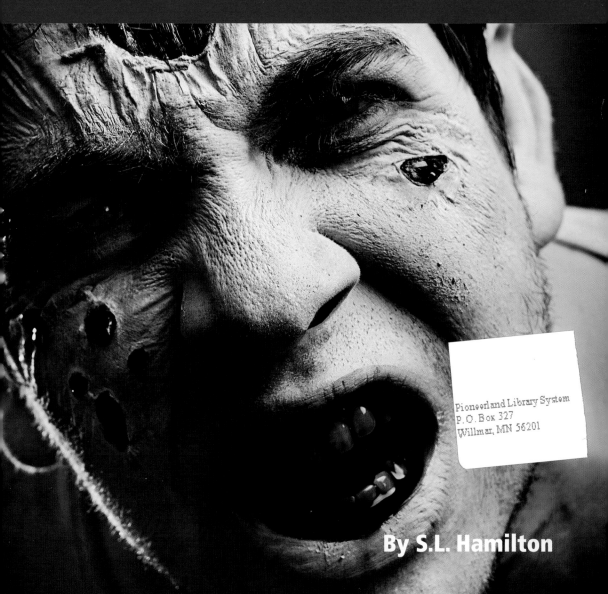

By S.L. Hamilton

VISIT US AT
WWW.ABDOPUBLISHING.COM

Published by ABDO Publishing Company, 8000 West 78th Street, Suite 310, Edina, MN 55439. Copyright ©2011 by Abdo Consulting Group, Inc. International copyrights reserved in all countries. No part of this book may be reproduced in any form without written permission from the publisher. A&D Xtreme™ is a trademark and logo of ABDO Publishing Company.

Printed in the United States of America, North Mankato, Minnesota.
052010
092010

 PRINTED ON RECYCLED PAPER

Editor: John Hamilton
Graphic Design: Sue Hamilton
Cover Design: John Hamilton
Cover Photo: Getty Images
Interior Photos: Alamy-pgs 16, 17, 18 & 19; AP-pg 32; Artfire Films-pg 26; Blank of the Dead Productions-pg 26; Capcom-pg 28; Columbia Pictures-pg 27; Corbis-pgs 8, 9, 10, 11 & 26; Crown Publishers-pg 29; Dead Films Inc-pg 26; George A. Romero-pg 26; Getty Images-pgs 30 & 31; Image Ten-pg 26; iStockphoto-pgs 1, 3, 4, 5, 20 & 21; Granger Collection-pgs 6 & 7; Laurel Group-pg 26; Marvel Entertainment Inc-pg 29; Mary Evans Picture Library-pgs 24 & 25; Peter Arnold-pgs 12, 13, 14 & 15; Photo Researchers-pgs 22 & 23; Thinkstock-pg 20; Three Rivers Press-pg 29; Universal Pictures-pgs 26 & 27; Valve-pg 28.

Library of Congress Cataloging-in-Publication Data

Hamilton, Sue L., 1959-
   Zombies / S.L. Hamilton.
      p. cm. -- (Xtreme monsters)
   Includes index.
   ISBN 978-1-61613-472-3
   1. Zombies--Juvenile literature. I. Title.
   GR581.H36 2011
   398'.45--dc22
                              2010002745

CONTENTS

XTREME

Zombies are neither dead nor alive. They are called walking corpses or members of the undead. With no will of their own, zombies walk the earth, living on human brains and body parts. Some are killers. Others are uncomplaining

ZOMBIES

ZOMBIE

African slaves brought the religion of voodoo and the concept of zombies to the island of Haiti, which was a busy slave center in the 1700s.

HISTORY

Many Haitian plantation owners feared slaves who practiced voodoo, often selling them to owners in North America.

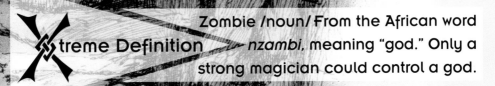

Xtreme Definition   Zombie /noun/ From the African word *nzambi*, meaning "god." Only a strong magician could control a god.

Cures and Curses

With the arrival of African and Haitian slaves, the ports of New Orleans, Louisiana, and Charleston, South Carolina, became voodoo centers. People of all skin colors visited voodoo priests and priestesses. They sought spells, potions, and charms for everything from love and health to bad luck and death.

Xtreme Definition

Gris-Gris /noun/ An African or Caribbean charm or piece of jewelry used in voodoo rituals.

Voodoo King

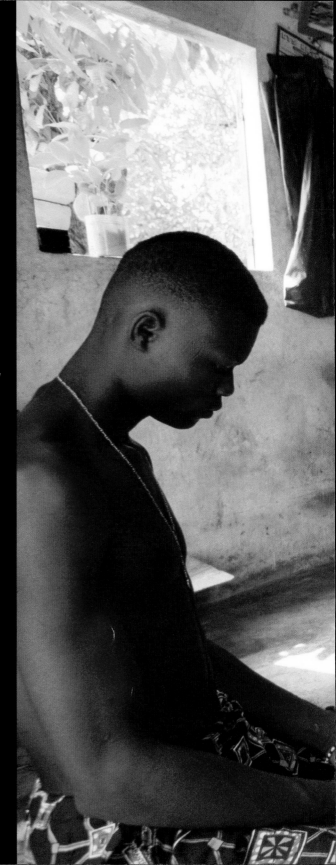

In the 1800s, one of the most famous voodoo kings was Dr. John Montenet. He was a tall, tattooed man of color. His New Orleans home was filled with herbs, bones, snakes, toads, and charms. People thought his powers were real. Dr. John even had his own staff of slaves. Many believed they were zombies.

A modern juju priest performs a traditional voodoo ceremony.

BLACK

MAGIC

Can a person be turned into a zombie?
Some say it can be done through the
power of suggestion. If a person believes
it can happen, it does. Others believe it
takes the skill of a black magician. Also
called a bokor, the magician uses powerful
drugs and poisons to control victims.

Xtreme Fact — Once in a trance, either through drugs or hypnotism, people may be controlled.

Pufferfish and Toads

Cane Toad

Nature provides ingredients that may turn people into zombies. If eaten, the eyes and internal organs of a pufferfish may result in paralysis and death. A marine toad, also called a cane toad, produces a highly toxic poison from glands behind its head. The poison may cause people to have no will of their own. It can also cause death.

STRENGTHS AND

Zombies do not feel pain. They never sleep or become tired. They fear nothing. They do not breathe, so they can survive underwater. Zombies have powerful teeth, which they use to rip and tear apart the flesh of living humans.

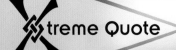 **Xtreme Quote**

"You've got red on you."
~*Shaun of the Dead*

WEAKNESSES

Weaknesses

Although tireless, zombies are slow. However, they often attack by the hundreds. If a tasty human is found, zombies will swarm around the unfortunate victim. Zombies may have difficulty turning a doorknob or opening a window, but they never stop trying. If a human tries to escape, zombies will surround and attack from all sides.

Xtreme Quote "Well-fed zombies will stick to the nutritious brain and bone marrow, leaving the rest of the viscera for the weaker members of the pack." ~Zombie Sociology

KILLING

A zombie can survive severe damage to its body. Even if it is cut in half, a zombie will attack. The only way a zombie can be killed is to destroy its brain. To be sure it's dead, the corpse should also be burned.

A ZOMBIE

REAL-LIFE

A medical condition called yaws causes disfiguring sores on a victim's face, legs, arms, and feet. Although 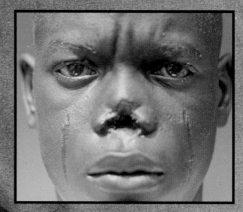 easily curable with modern antibiotics, many people are never treated. Their deformities may have led people to believe they were seeing zombies.

ZOMBIES

Felicia Felix-Mentor

Felicia Felix-Mentor was a woman who died in Haiti in 1907. In 1936, an older woman who looked like Felicia reappeared in her village. She was short and lame, as Felicia had been. However, she was starving and could not speak properly. Her diseased eyes were sensitive to sunlight. Many believed she was the zombie of Felicia.

Doctors believed the "zombie" woman was a mentally ill person who simply looked like Felicia.

ZOMBIE

George A. Romero's *Night of the Living Dead* is the film from which most modern zombie movies have their roots. In this 1968 film, radiation from a fallen satellite brings the dead back to eat the living. Romero created several sequels.

MOVIES

In 2009's *Zombieland*, human survivors of a zombie apocalypse take a road trip in search of a zombie-free area.

Shaun of the Dead is a "rom zom com" (romantic zombie comedy) featuring Shaun, a zombie-hunting salesman.

ZOMBIE GAMES

Zombies are the subject of several video games. Most of these games pit humans against hoards of undead zombies.

One man versus a mall full of zombies.

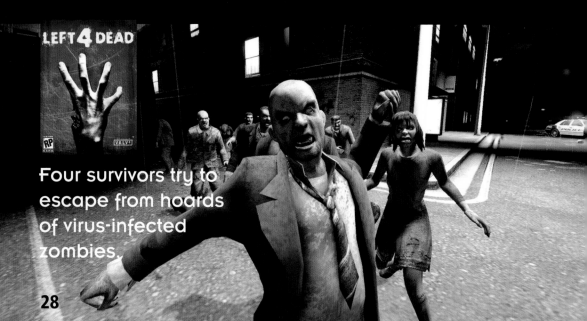

Four survivors try to escape from hoards of virus-infected zombies.

AND BOOKS

Written by Max Brooks, these fictional books give details on surviving a zombie uprising, and encounters with zombies.

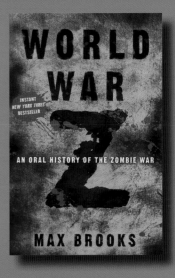

Marvel Comics' superheroes became the most powerful zombies ever to eat human brains in this 2005-2006 series.

THE

Antibiotics
Powerful medicines that kill harmful bacteria in the body.

Apocalypse
An event resulting in severe damage or total destruction of the world.

Bokor
A practitioner of black magic capable of creating zombies.

Corpse
A dead body.

Haiti
An island in the Caribbean. It was a busy slave center in the 1700s.

Juju
Supernatural powers given to a charm or other object

GLOSSARY

Paralysis
An inability, either physically or mentally, to move one's body.

Ritual
A religious or serious ceremony where specific actions are conducted in a certain order.

Viscera
Organs inside the body, such as the stomach and intestines.

Voodoo
A religion begun in Haiti by slaves brought from Africa. It combines elements of many religions, and uses rites from several ethnic groups. One type of voodoo includes the practice of zombification.

INDEX